This Ladybird Book belongs to:

_____

_____

_____

_____

D1355741

This Ladybird retelling
by
Audrey Daly

Ladybird books are widely available, but in case of
difficulty may be ordered by post or telephone from:

Ladybird Books – Cash Sales Department
Littlegate Road Paignton Devon TQ3 3BE
Telephone 0803 554761

A catalogue record for this book is available
from the British Library

First edition

Published by Ladybird Books Ltd Loughborough Leicestershire UK
Ladybird Books Inc Auburn Maine 04210 USA

© LADYBIRD BOOKS LTD MCMXCIII

All rights reserved. No part of this publication may be reproduced,
stored in a retrieval system, or transmitted in any form or by any
means, electronic, mechanical, photocopying, recording or otherwise,
without the prior consent of the copyright owner.

LADYBIRD TINY TALES

Goldilocks
and the
Three Bears

illustrated
by
CHRIS RUSSELL

based on a traditional folk tale

Once upon a time, there were three bears who lived in a little house right in the middle of the forest.

There was great big Father Bear, and medium-sized Mother Bear, and little tiny Baby Bear.

Honey

One morning, Mother Bear made a big pot of porridge and put it into three bowls for breakfast.

But the porridge was much too hot to eat.

"We will leave it to cool while we go for our early morning walk," said Father Bear. "When we come back, it will be just right." So off they went into the forest.

Nearby there lived a very naughty, mischievous little girl. She was called Goldilocks because she had long, golden hair.

That morning, as she was passing the three bears' house, Goldilocks saw that the front door was open.

"I'll just have a little peep inside," she said to herself.

As soon as she saw the porridge, naughty Goldilocks rushed over to taste it. "I do feel rather hungry," she said.

But the porridge in Father Bear's
big bowl was still too hot. And the
porridge in Mother Bear's
medium-sized bowl was lumpy.

At last Goldilocks tried Baby
Bear's porridge. It was just right,
so she ate up every spoonful!

After that, Goldilocks decided that she would like to sit down. But Father Bear's big chair was much too high.

Next she sat in Mother Bear's medium-sized chair. "This one is much too hard!" she grumbled.

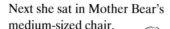

At last she found Baby Bear's tiny chair. It wasn't too high. It wasn't too hard. It was just right!

Goldilocks leaned back happily in
Baby Bear's chair. But she was far
too heavy. With a *creak* and a
crack, the chair fell to pieces.

Bump! Goldilocks landed in a
heap on the floor. "Well, really!"
she said crossly. "I've had such a
shock, I shall have to lie down."

So Goldilocks went upstairs. She tried Father Bear's big bed, but that was far too hard.

And Mother Bear's medium-sized bed was far too soft!

"Now this *is* comfortable," sighed Goldilocks, settling into Baby Bear's little bed. And she fell fast asleep!

Before long, the three bears
arrived home from their walk.

"I'm ready for my breakfast *right
now,*" said Father Bear. But when
he got to the table he cried out in
surprise, "Someone's been eating
my porridge!"

"And someone's been eating *my* porridge," said Mother Bear. "I wonder why they didn't like it?"

"They must have liked mine!" cried Baby Bear, holding his empty bowl. "Someone's been eating my porridge, and they've eaten it all up!"

"Look!" said Father Bear. "Someone's been sitting in my chair!"

"And someone's been sitting in *my* chair," said Mother Bear.

"Someone's been sitting in my chair," sobbed poor little Baby Bear, "and they've broken it to pieces!"

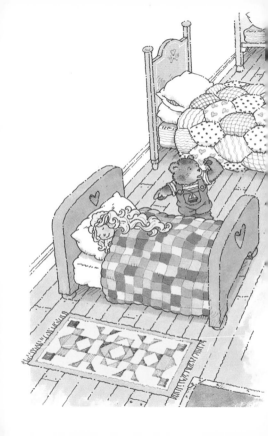

The three bears began to search the house. Upstairs, Father Bear looked around. "Someone's been sleeping in my bed!" he said.

"And someone's been sleeping in *my* bed," cried Mother Bear.

"Oh!" squeaked Baby Bear. "Someone's been sleeping in my bed and she's *still here!*"

At the sound of Baby Bear's voice, Goldilocks woke up. The first thing she saw was Father Bear, looking very cross.

Goldilocks jumped up in fright.
She ran down the stairs and out of
the house as fast as she could.

"I don't think she'll trouble us
again," said Father Bear, smiling.

And she never did.